T·H·E

Twelve Dancing Princesses

T · H · E
Twelve Dancing Princesses

retold and illustrated by

JANE RAY

Dutton Children's Books

New York

for my sisters Elizabeth and Caroline, with much love

CIP Data is available.
Published in the United States 1996 by
Dutton Children's Books,
a division of Penguin Books USA Inc.
375 Hudson Street, New York, New York 10014
Originally published in Great Britain 1996 by
Orchard Children's Books, London
Typography by Julia Goodman
Printed in Belgium First American Edition
ISBN 0-525-45595-7
10 9 8 7 6 5 4 3 2 1

There was once a king who had twelve daughters, each one as clever and beautiful as the next. He loved them all dearly, but he was puzzled by something strange that occurred night after night.

Every evening, the king would kiss his daughters good night and settle them down to sleep in the long bedchamber they shared. Then he would tiptoe away, taking care to lock and bolt the door behind him.

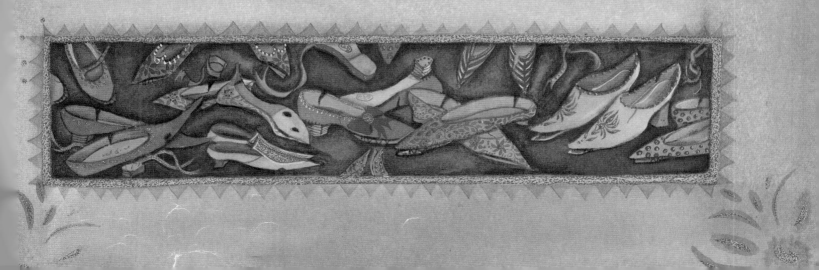

Yet every morning the princesses were tired and wan, and their silken dancing shoes were in shreds. Where did they go each night? the king wondered. And how did they leave their room? He was determined to solve the mystery. For one thing, twelve new pairs of satin dancing slippers a day were costing him a fortune!

The princesses were certainly not telling, so the king issued a proclamation. The first man who discovered their secret would be allowed to choose one of the princesses to marry; and then he would rule the kingdom with her when the old king died. But he must solve the puzzle in three days and three nights or be banished from the kingdom forever.

Marry one of the beautiful princesses and become king! You can imagine that it wasn't long before most of the young men in the realm and beyond were lined up at the palace gates to try their luck.

The first to try was a king's son. He was led to a small dressing room next to the princesses' bedchamber. The prince was enchanted by the twelve beautiful young women and happily drank the wine the eldest offered him. Then, after the princesses had gone to their room, he made sure that their door was ajar and settled down to his nightlong vigil. But, however hard he struggled, the prince could not keep his eyes open. Soon he was gently snoring, and then suddenly it was

morning. The twelve princesses were in their bedchamber, sleeping soundly, and on the floor were the twelve pairs of worn-out dancing slippers.

The second night, the prince drank the same sweet wine, felt the same overwhelming need to sleep, and realized in the morning that he had failed. The third night was no different. The young prince was duly banished from the kingdom, and another suitor took up the challenge.

It was the same for that one, too, and for the rest who tried. The king was in despair. Were his daughters to outwit every man in the kingdom?

Some time later a poor soldier, returning wounded from battle, sat down to rest by the side of the road. He was enjoying a simple meal of bread and cheese when an old woman approached. Because the soldier was a kind man, he offered her half of his food.

"Where are you heading?" the old woman asked. The soldier laughed. "Off to try my luck at the palace," he said. "Can't you just imagine me as king!" he joked.

But the old woman remained serious. "Don't touch the wine those clever girls offer you. Just pretend to drink. Likewise pretend to fall asleep. And take this cloak. If you put it on, it will make you invisible, and you can follow them wherever they go."

The soldier was puzzled, but he thanked the strange old woman, took the cloak, and set off for the palace.

Though the king had given up hope of discovering his daughters' secret, he greeted the soldier courteously and decided to give him a chance. And so when bedtime came, the soldier was led to the small room next to the princesses' bedchamber. The eldest princess offered him a cup of wine. The soldier pretended to sip . . . and to sip some more. The wine did not run down his throat, however, but into a small sponge he had cleverly tied under his chin.

Then, as if overcome with tiredness, the soldier yawned loudly and rolled over onto his bed. "Silly fool," scoffed the eldest princess. And, laughing merrily, the twelve sisters twirled into their room to prepare for the night ahead.

They flung open their cupboards and trunks and began to dress themselves in
fine lace and linen, embroidered silk, and rich velvet and brocade. They curled
and plaited each other's hair, painted lips, powdered faces, and ruffled fans.
Finally every princess slipped on a new pair of dancing shoes. . . .

Only the youngest could not enjoy herself. "Something feels amiss tonight," she said. But her eldest sister, impatient to be off, told her not to be a silly goose, and clapped her hands three times. A door appeared in the wall. Slowly it swung open, and the twelve princesses disappeared through it.

The soldier clambered from his bed and hurried after them, flinging his magic cloak around his shoulders as he went. In his haste, he stumbled and stepped on the hem of the youngest princess's dress. "What was that?" she cried. "Someone is following us. I know something's not right tonight."

"Nonsense," said her eldest
sister. But the youngest sensed
something wrong all the same,
and she kept looking back as
they made their way down
flights of stairs and along the
corridors. Finally the princesses
arrived at the entranceway to a
lush garden.

The soldier drew his breath—he had never seen such a magical place.

The princesses hurried through the silvery trees, which glimmered softly in the moonlight.

They came to a garden of gold, where plump, delicious fruits hung down from burnished branches. Crossing this, they stepped through an arch of roses into a third garden all of diamonds, which sparkled and shimmered in the dark like a spangled sky of stars.

In each garden, the soldier felt he must be dreaming and reached up to snap
off a twig, just to be sure. Each time, the noise startled the youngest princess;
but each time, her sisters just laughed away her fears and hurried her on.

An avenue of diamond-studded trees led down to a lake, and there on the water bobbed twelve little painted boats. In each sat a handsome prince, waiting to row the princesses across the water.

The soldier was by now growing used to this strange, enchanted world. Taking care to cover himself with his magical cloak, he climbed into the boat with the youngest princess.

After a while, the prince rowing the boat stopped to rest. "Why is the boat so slow tonight when I'm rowing as hard as I always do?"

The youngest sister only shivered in reply. Across the lake stood a wonderful castle. Lights shone from every window, fireworks exploded in the sky above, and the sound of drums and trumpets, flutes and violins reached down to the lake, urging all to join the party.

The princesses ran up to the castle and danced with their princes all through the night. They ate the most mouthwatering foods and drank the finest wines.

The soldier, safe within his cloak, danced also, weaving among the couples and even stealing morsels of food out from under the noses of the unsuspecting guests. Once, feeling very bold, he took a sip from the youngest princess's goblet.

"Now someone is tasting my drink," she exclaimed, almost in tears.

But her eldest sister, whirling past, only laughed. "Oh, do stop worrying and come dance. We've only a few hours left."

And sure enough, their slippers were soon so worn through that they could not be danced in a minute longer. It was time for the princesses to go home.

The princes rowed the sisters back across the lake, and this time the soldier traveled in the boat with the eldest princess. All the young women were beautiful, each in her own way, but to him the eldest was the most interesting.

The princesses promised to meet their princes the following night, and then they hurried back through the three gardens and along the palace passageways.

Now they were truly tired. While they wearily climbed the last flight of stairs, the soldier slipped past them in his cloak. By the time the princesses peeped in his door, he was lying in bed, snoring gently, apparently fast asleep.

"Silly fool!" said the eldest princess. "Our secret is still safe." And she lingered a moment, watching him as he slept.

◆　◆　◆

The next morning the soldier felt sure it had all been a dream, in spite of the three twigs he had picked from the gardens. He decided to keep his vigil once more before telling the king what he had discovered. The second night went exactly like the first.

In fact, the soldier enjoyed himself so much he couldn't resist following the princesses for a third night of dancing and feasting. This last time, as further proof, he came away with a golden goblet under his cloak.

On the fourth morning, the king wearily summoned the soldier to his study. The sisters hid outside the door to hear what the young man had to say and how he would fare.

"Have you discovered how my daughters wear out their slippers every night?" asked the king.

"I have, your majesty," replied the soldier. "They dance away the night in an underground castle, with twelve handsome princes." And as he explained about the hidden door, the three gardens, the lake, and the castle, he produced from his pockets the three twigs and the golden goblet.

The king called for each of his daughters in turn, beginning with the youngest, and asked whether the soldier's story was true. Each princess hung her head in silence until at last the eldest was questioned. "Father, it's true," she replied. "The soldier has outwitted us."

"Then you must decide which of my daughters you wish to marry," the king said to the soldier. The soldier knew that he had already chosen the eldest. And when she saw that he was kind as well as clever, she was pleased to accept. "Provided we can have plenty of dancing at the wedding," she said with a smile.

The wedding took place soon afterward, and everyone
who came danced the night away.

When, some time later, the old king died, the princess and the soldier ruled the kingdom together fairly and happily for many years.

As queen, the eldest sister decreed that she and her sisters should go dancing as often and as late into the night as they wished. And, just to be sure, she appointed a royal shoemaker to keep their dancing shoes in good repair.